From
The
Shadows

E.J. Stevens

Sacred Oaks Press

Published by Sacred Oaks Press
Sacred Oaks, 221 Sacred Oaks Lane, Wells, Maine 04090

First Printing (trade paperback edition), September 2009

Stevens, E.J.
From the Shadows / E.J. Stevens

ISBN 978-0-9842475-0-9 (trade pbk.)

Printed in the United States of America

PUBLISHER'S NOTE
This is a work of fiction. Names, characters, places, and
incidents either are the product of the author's imagination
or are used fictitiously, and any resemblance to actual
persons, living or dead, business establishments, events, or
locales is entirely coincidental.

To my family.
Mom and Dad I could not have completed
this without your constant love and support.

To my friends.
Byron, Nathaniel, Bill, Kaitlyn, Chris, Franka,
Susie & Pete.
Thank you for always believing.

Contents

On Sparrow's Wings

Graveyard Whispers

Shadow Queen of the Sidhe

Blackberry lips
Brimstone embers in her hair
The evil temptress beckons
For you to come into her lair

Feet dancing on the dark crags
Legs bare but for swirling mist
She pouts at your indecision
And offers up a kiss

Wrapped in shifting shadows
She sways from side to side
Looks coyly through dark lashes
Opens her mouth wide

A growl escapes her
As she reaches for your face
Shadow Queen of the Sidhe
Wraps you in her dark embrace

Haunted (by my Alice)

Who is Alice?

I remember tea parties in the garden

dancing until our legs were sore

You let me wear your blue dress

the one I used to adore

Where are you Alice?

You sat there in the parlor

cutting finger sandwiches on the parquet floor

smearing cream cheese on the walls

dumping tea into the drawers

What happened to my Alice?

Is that you behind the door?

I remember tying bows and ribbons

then finding them on the floor

still holding clumps of golden hair

You didn't want to brush it anymore

Are you out there Alice?
Still fighting your little war
You said to call you Alex
Alice's death I'll ever mourn
Your love was all that mattered
but you looked at me with naked scorn

How could you take away my Alice?
Revenge for you I swore
now the dress is torn and tattered
from running through the thorns

Sometimes I hear you Alice
Your voice I can't ignore
Your words are full of malice
the blood I spilt that day was yours.

Graveyard Whispers

Their whispers rise up
From below ground
Rustle through the leaves
Over each burial mound

Around headstones of marble and granite
Clawing up through the dirt
Moaning their regrets and sorrows
Sobbing of grief and hurt

Whistle through the treetops
Past monuments cast in stone
Resonates through their caskets
Rattling cloth and bone

Whispers of broken promises
Head begins to pound
As my mind fills with their whispers
Sighing up from below the ground

The Fallen Ones

The Fallen Ones
Reign over bones
Of loves lost
And lovers scorned

Enshrined by monuments
So dire
And licked by flames
Of hell fire

Once they touched
Heaven's Gates
But their tale is one
Of lust and fate

For their devotion wrought
Great jealousy
And their behavior
Still evokes heresy

For they loved to the point
Of obsession
And fought for
God's own possession

Everlasting bleeding scars
And splintered wings
Remain in this domain
Barbed wire and sinew hold
Together this flesh of pain

The damaged and anointed ones
Who are forever bound
By twine, bracken and love
Never to leave Holy ground.

The Boatman Below

Duck my head
As I enter
The ceilings are low

Fingers trailing
Damp brickwork
Feel my way as I go

To seek out
The boatman
The Boatman Below

Descend
Pain darkened stairways
My footsteps echo

Wings brush by
In the black
A bat or a crow

The musty smell
Rushes to me
Fitful wind does blow

These effluvium
filled waters
Mix with tides ebb and flow

Creating the murky stage
Upon which
The boatman will row

He appears with a
Flash of his shark teeth
Laughing demon eyes glow

I stumble to him
In silence
Feeling weak and hollow

His hand snakes out
To grab me
There is nowhere to go

He dances with glee
And sways
To and fro

While he sups from
This chalice
Of pain and sorrow.

Shadow Man

Shadowy man
With hat and cane
I used to love you so

But you turned my love
Into a game
Resentment you did sow

You fed me your lips
And supped on my pain
Letting my hatred for you grow

You dueled with words
And cutting remarks
But what you didn't know

Was that your cruelty
Released me from your spell
Now friend had become foe.

Child Catcher

Poets weep
And children sleep
Your pocket-watch keeps the time

Grasping hands
And holding nets
Cages filled with grime

But some things even
You can't hold
My heart, my soul, my mind

Someday soon
I'll snuff you out
By my hand you'll die

Then they'll crown
A new Child Catcher
My name I'll cast aside

For now I know
Of nothing else
But the need to survive

So I'll hoard my treasure
And await the day
I visit the place I've locked inside.

Seeker of the Grail

Climb up the hills
To fairy glade
Deep in the forest behind the veil
The mists do part
Upon swirling leaves I sail

Through time and place
History unmade
The mind does grasp and flail
Crashes on rocks of solid truth
And reaches for the Grail

Eyes alight with fever's gleam
Hair so quickly grayed
Skin gone sickly pale
Hands shake near constantly
Inside their rusty mail

Only one who is worthy
With Heaven's aid
Bearing the one True Cross
Complete with blood and nail
Can enter without affliction
And take up the Holy Grail.

Plague Rats

They come up from the sewers
Skitter up pipes and stone
A mass exodus from the darkness
Spreading out towards your home

They brush past you while you're sleeping
Infecting you as they go
Searching for crumbs and feeding
Before returning to their homes below

Satisfied with full bellies
They leave death in their wake
Hundreds of innocent families
Who will never awake

For those who do awaken
It will be only to nightmare
Of blackened flesh and open sores
That lead them to despair

Laying helpless in their beds

Gasping wetly for breath

Prayers pass cracked lips

Hoping for the release of death.

Chronos

Chronos comes
To change an age
Pens the time
And turns the page

He winds the clocks
He checks the gears
Pulls on his gloves
As a new era nears

He dons his hat
And grabs his cane
As we reach the end
Another monarch's reign

The last grains of sand
Fall through the glass
This day too
Soon shall pass

Chronos gathers his cloak
As the final grains descend
For the time has come
For it all to end.

Nocturne and Lunarius

Dare approach the gates we wrought
With fire and with blood
Across war ravaged barren wastes
Through seas of corpse and mud

Scale trenches carved by giants
Climb scorched bone and wood
To the monument of our hearts vanity
A home that never could

Contain immortal passions and jealousy
A marriage often misunderstood
Lunarius shining in the sky
Nocturne shadowed within her hood.

Tower of My Despair

This endless siege
Upon my senses
Locked in the tower
Of my despair

Expecting terror
In deep shadows
Yet love's assassins
Are not there

Poisoned blades
Need only prick
For doubt
To bind and snare

To truly avoid
Its taint
One must
Take every care

Hide away
From your affections
Build walls
High up in the air

Shield my heart
Behind brick and mortar
Locked in the tower
Of my despair.

Madness

I'm the cluster of shadows
chill breeze on your neck
the ache in your stomach
that makes you feel sick

You might try to see me
but cast all your bones
no way can you find me
I hide in your home

You twist and you whisper
you mutter you groan
you call out for salvation
but find you're alone

You shake with a chill
but you're covered in sweat
I will come to get you
just haven't come yet

You sway and you falter
your life such a mess
but you find yourself in
your favorite silk dress

I betray and I bother
I cast out my net
to capture you darling
my own marionette

Now tied up in strings
and covered in knots
you struggle but fail
it's worse than you thought

You twist and you whisper
you mutter you groan
you call out for salvation
but find you're alone.

Modern Wasteland

Scars

I worry at the scars
Beneath my fingers
The skin beneath my hands
Each bump a hesitation
Every ridge a new demand

Skin looks melted like the candle
That has burned for hours
You visit me at my sick bed
But you do not bring me flowers

I wonder idly what that means
But it's difficult to care
I ride this cloud of morphine
From bliss back to despair

These scars have somehow
Changed me
Left their mark upon my skin
No matter if you touch me
I'll never be the same again.

Behind the Mask

Woman in the mirror
Girl behind the mask
Who are you really?
I'm not afraid to ask

Cut down through the layers
To raw unfettered skin
Look past the masks we wear
To the true person within

Discard the lies that chain you
Peer past the glamour and the veil
From behind which stalks your beast
The fear that you will fail

It watches from the shadows
Always on the prowl
Stifling flickers of confidence
With a warning growl

So you hide behind the mask
Take the image of the beast
While looking out with frightened eyes
On others pain you feast

But ruled by your fear
You wish for release at last
Woman in the mirror
Girl behind the glass.

Modern Wasteland

The hum of power lines
Pounding behind my eyes
Their cat's cradle silhouette
Black against the sky

Vampiric fluorescent light bulbs
Sucking at my soul
Bleeding me of my very essence
Making me prematurely old

Tapping of fingers on keyboards
Tappity-tap-tap-click
Creating staccato induced vertigo
So dizzy I am sick

Stark skyscraper outline
A horizon of broken teeth
Sunset on the skyline
Places bleeding gums beneath

In this modern wasteland
It is difficult to find
Another who shares ones passions
Of heart and soul and mind

This misbegotten landscape
Our future torn asunder
Crackles with heat lighting
Rumbles with constant thunder

In this desert of our hearts
On this highway through the sand
Stumble mindless zombies
Through our modern wasteland.

Reign Me In

No one can tame me

No one

Can reign me in

Might be fun to try

But you know

You cannot win

No one can tame me

No one

Can reign me in

Like a wild thing

In the night

Fever gleam

On my skin

No one can tame me

No one

Can reign me in.

E.J. Stevens

The Visitors

They come
They come for me
They come for me in the night
With their light that shines so wrongly
The light that shines so bright

With their raven's heads and sparrow's wings
They glide across the floor
Lower half buried beneath their cloaks
I can't bear to see more

But the darkness behind my eyes
Is even more frightening still
So I look out again at these visitors
Who hold me against my will

I recoil from their inspection
But I cannot run from here
I seem to be frozen in place
With this realization comes more fear

They tilt their heads too far for human necks
As if I were some curiosity
But perhaps for them I am just a puzzle
Like the crosswords I mull over with my tea

Their black beady eyes seem to absorb all light
And I find myself falling into those beads of black
While some part of me wonders idly
If they've come here for a snack

But when I awake to find myself intact
I cannot remember why this should concern me
As I take my shower and eat breakfast
I rush off for another workday in a hurry

But I pull up short as a bird flies past me
Swooping into its nearby nest
As I watch it twist its head on its neck
I feel tonight I won't get much rest.

Trapped In My Skin

My scar burns today
Aching for what might have been
Would things have been better
Who's to say
Am I somehow paying for my sins?

A penance for my lack of faith
Twist me, break me but I will not bend
There has to be a better way
Violated by physicians again and again
Trapped in here day after day
How can I forgive He who created Them?

Someday I'll make you pay
Peel back the layers and stitch you in
No way to express, no words I can say
For you to understand
What it is to be trapped in my skin.

Plato Was Right

Been content here
Just me
On my own

Didn't need
A prince charming
To save me
From being alone

But Plato was right
All along
There is someone
Out there
The other half
Of my Form

How suddenly
You complete me
How swiftly
You can sweep me
Into your arms

Plato was right
All along
I am a circle
That's been torn.

Sucking on Pennies

I'm so cold
But they say that's normal
I can't move
They tell me not to worry

There's a bad taste in my mouth
But I'm not sucking on pennies
There's a ghost in my throat
Or maybe a banshee
Since she wants to scream
But she's cold to the bone
So cold and alone
And frozen like me
Just like me

Just like me
You want to scream
Like me
Just like me
You're caught in a dream
Like me
Just like me

I'm so cold

But they say that's normal

I can't remember

How did I get here?

I can't move

They won't let me out

There's a bad taste in my mouth

But I'm not sucking on pennies

There's a ghost in my throat

Or maybe a banshee

Since she wants to scream

But she's cold to the bone

So cold and alone

And frozen like me

Just like me

Just like me

You want to scream

Like me

Just like me

You're caught in a dream

Like me

Just like me

I'm so cold

I can feel something hot pouring out

I can't move

I just want to scream and shout

whisper but nothing comes out.

Dowager's Black Dress

Dowager in her black dress
Faded from years of pain
Keeps eyes on her wet boots
Avoids gray faces in the rain

Seeing their pity would bring disaster
She steadily avoids their eyes
Lets the storm rage in her bosom
Like this weeping from the skies

Whispers behind their hands
Form the bars of her cage
Their smiles and their laughter
Fill her with rage

Forever living in the shadows
Always on her own
Never to be included
Condemned to be alone

Bites her lip before it trembles

Quiet tears blend with the rain

Dowager in her black dress

Faded from years of pain.

Sanctuary

It is always so very quiet here
A place to hide from the pain and fear
Moss and lichen covered stone
Cast the illusion that I am all alone

With spongy moss beneath my feet
All I can hear is my own heartbeat
Yet behind these walls of stone and oak
Are many who have donned the cloak

I wonder again if I am truly ready
Then remember the intense joy so heady
Yes, I do believe its time
To approach these walls streaked with lime

My hand shakes as I reach the door
But I brace myself and knock once more
A beatific face smiles up at me
Nods and gestures for my entry

As I cross into the tiny courtyard

I am reminded of the words of a famous bard

"To truly live a life of piety

One must remove oneself from society"

The first time I heard this I didn't agree

I felt that above all one must be free

But life has a funny way of changing ones thoughts

And I considered what my life of freedom had wrought

Too much suffering, pain and above all regret

So I would come to the brothers to forget

The silence of this place is a soothing balm

My frenetic mind replaced with calm

They never questioned how long I would stay

And each time I felt the urge I would be on my way

How many times have I come here over the years

Seeking an escape from my worries and fears

They never tried to stop me when I would leave

Though their eyes would turn sad and they would grieve

Today they must know that I've decided to stay

For they all nod and smile peacefully as they look my way

I am struck by their love and total acceptance
Which they convey without uttering a single sentence
I am now certain that I have made the correct choice
Even though no one will ever again hear my voice

I will make my vow and don my cloak
My former identity drifting away like smoke
I believe that now I can finally cope
In this place of solace and of hope.

On Sparrow's Wings

My Mother's Garden

There is a heady scent of plants and humus earth

Beneath the kitchen window sill

Where you will find my mother's garden

My refuge since I were little

A whisper of autumn on the breeze

Is cool enough to chill

But the sparrow preening in the sun

Believes its summer still

Herbs both sweet and savory in their rows

All dancing to her will

I breathe in those that were my mother's favorites

Lavender, sage and dill

She may be gone these long years past

But she remains here still.

Apple Tree's Lament

You hailed the coachman
To stop your carriage
Here.

You gazed upon my laden boughs
With your heavy lidded
leer.

The serpent traveled up my trunk
And carried my own
Fear.

You tore away my fruit that day
Shot me your crooked
Sneer.

You spit out our apple seeds
Without shedding a single
Tear.

My grief runs deep through sap and root
The future now looks
Drear.

You strode away so long ago
But your memory is always
Near.

Even now leaves fall to the ground
At this very time of
Year.

On Sparrow's Wings

On Sparrow's Wings
All our dreams take flight
Goldfinches eating thistle
Feathers shining bright

The whisper of dragonflies
Bring about childish delight
Doves cooing to each other
In the days fading light

Raven's silhouette
Causes a shiver at twilight
A murder of crows descend
Bringing with them blackest night.

Your Kiss is a Riptide

You are
The clouds that mask the moon
The mist across my eyes
The veil beneath my brow
A storm surge at sunrise

You
Churn these ocean waters
Leaving no place for me to hide
I gasp for air but find your lips
Your kiss is a riptide

You drag me to the bottom
I cannot find the sky
When I swim in your dark waters
The only light is in your eyes
I try to find the surface
To escape the things you hide
But I'm swept into your vortex
Your waves I long to ride

You
Churn these ocean waters
Leaving no place for me to hide
I gasp for air but find your lips
Your kiss is a riptide

This liquid languid love affair
Atop your waves I drift and glide
I could stay like this forever
But then I turn onto my side
Pulled down into this whirlpool
When I look into your eyes

You
Churn these ocean waters
Leaving no place for me to hide
I gasp for air but find your lips
Your kiss is a riptide.

Betwixt and Between

The veil descends
A dew filled mist
Enshrouds the night

Laying its clammy hands
Upon me
Creating such a fright

Cast a fog
Across my vision
Stealing away my sight

Owls hoot their haunting calls
Wolves slink quietly
Through the night.

Waterfall's Descent

Tears pour into me
Against my will
Pushing me further
Down this hill

Belly roiling, churning
I vomit up your crying
Can't you stop this spinning
I think it might be worth dying

Can't break the surface
No way to touch you now
So I'll just wrap my arms
around your memory
And take this leap
Tonight

Smash against the rocks

Of destiny

Smash into tree and stone

I will take you with me

To the very bottom

Of my soul.

Farewell Sparrow

Alight upon the fence rails
Flitting to and fro

Searching for your dinner
Through rain and sun and snow

My darling little sparrow
How I love you so

Since you were just a tiny chick
I have watched you grow

Soon you will leave my garden
I know not where you'll go.

Dichotomy

I have this dream

Where I float upon the river

'I am the River'

The sunlight blinds my open eyes

'Moonlight dances on my surface'

Everything so painfully vivid

'It's dark down here'

So wonderfully clear

'Murky and distorted'

Musical sound of bubbling water

'Deafening silence'

Like laughter on the breeze

'Shedding tears forever'

Float away

'Flow away'

From all the pain

'From those I loved'

To a place of calm

'To a certain death'

Losing myself along the way

'Losing myself along the way'.

The Curious Little Sparrow

Said the sparrow to the nightingale
"Why is your song so sad?"
But the nightingale didn't answer
Which made the sparrow mad

Little sparrow puffed out his chest
And exclaimed, "I didn't want to know!"
Then flew over to the oak tree
And landed beside the crow

The sparrow then asked the crow
"Why do crows travel in a flock?"
Rather than answer him the crow flew away
Which was rather quite a shock

"Hmpf!" went sparrow feeling embarrassed anger
"I'll go ask that bright fellow the tananger"
The scarlet tananger was easy to find
Since he was a very bright shade of red
"Mr. Tananger" asked the sparrow
"Why are your wings not the color of your head?"

Well perhaps it was a rude question
Only another tananger would know
But he flew away from sparrow
Who took it as quite a blow

"No one wishes to talk to me"
Sparrow cried alone on his perch
Then came a beautiful trilling
From the branch of a peeling birch

The sparrow went to take a look
And met with a wonderful surprise
The bird here looked just like him
Even to his eyes

The sparrow shyly asked
"What kind of bird has such a lovely song?"
The female bird replied, "I am a sparrow like you!"
"Would you like to sing along?"

From that day forward our curious little sparrow
Never had to wait
For he got all his answers
From his lovely little mate.

Dancing With the Wind

The wind rushes across the trees
Who lean into its soft caress

While the stirring of the leaves
Sounds like a lover sighing "yes"

The wind slows to an idle breeze
And stills the swaying branches

Yet the leaves swirling at their knees
Continue with their fitful dances.

Gears, Steam & Absinthe Daydreams

Coming to Amazon

Fall 2010.

Sacred Oaks Press

ABOUT THE AUTHOR

E. J. Stevens is a graduate of the University of Maine at
Farmington with a Bachelor of Arts in Psychology.

Erica has worked in a variety of jobs that demonstrate the human
condition including schools, psychiatric hospitals and (*shudder*)
shopping malls. She currently resides on the coast of Maine where
she finds daily inspiration for her writing.

www.ingramcontent.com/pod-product-compliance
Lightning Source LLC
Chambersburg PA
CBHW071224170626
46809CB00005BA/1924